My dearest puppy, Storm,

I hope this letter reaches you safe and sound. You have been so brave since you had to flee from the evil wolf Shadow.

Do not worry about me. I will hide here until you are strong enough to return and lead our pack. For now you must move on – you must hide from Shadow and his spies. If Shadow finds this letter I believe he will try to destroy it . . .

Find a good friend – someone to help finish my message to you. Because what I have to say to you is important. What I have to say is this: you must always

Please don't feel lonely. Trust in your friends and all will be well.

Your loving mother,

Canista

Sue Bentley's books for children often include animals, fairies and wildlife. She lives in Northampton and enjoys reading, going to the cinema, relaxing by her garden pond and watching the birds feeding their babies on the lawn. At school she was always getting told off for daydreaming or staring out of the window – but she now realizes that she was storing up ideas for when she became a writer. She has met and owned many cats and dogs and each one has brought a special kind of magic to her life.

Sue Bentley

Magic Puppy

Cloud Capers

Illustrated by *Angela Swan*

PUFFIN

To Ziggy – four-squat and ugly-cute,

but full of character

PUFFIN BOOKS

Published by the Penguin Group
Penguin Books Ltd, 80 Strand, London WC2R ORL, England
Penguin Group (USA) Inc., 375 Hudson Street, New York, New York 10014, USA
Penguin Group (Canada), 90 Eglinton Avenue East, Suite 700, Toronto, Ontario, Canada M4P 2Y3
(a division of Pearson Penguin Canada Inc.)
Penguin Ireland, 25 St Stephen's Green, Dublin 2, Ireland (a division of Penguin Books Ltd)
Penguin Group (Australia), 250 Camberwell Road, Camberwell, Victoria 3124, Australia
(a division of Pearson Australia Group Pty Ltd)
Penguin Books India Pvt Ltd, 11 Community Centre, Panchsheel Park, New Delhi – 110 017, India
Penguin Group (NZ), 67 Apollo Drive, Rosedale, North Shore 0632, New Zealand
(a division of Pearson New Zealand Ltd)
Penguin Books (South Africa) (Pty) Ltd, 24 Sturdee Avenue, Rosebank,
Johannesburg 2196, South Africa

Penguin Books Ltd, Registered Offices: 80 Strand, London WC2R ORL, England

puffinbooks.com

First published 2008
6

Text copyright © Sue Bentley, 2008
Illustrations copyright © Angela Swan, 2008
All rights reserved

The moral right of the author and illustrator has been asserted

Set in Bembo
Typeset by Palimpsest Book Production Limited, Grangemouth, Stirlingshire
Made and printed in England by Clays Ltd, St Ives plc

British Library Cataloguing in Publication Data
A CIP catalogue record for this book is available from the British Library

ISBN: 978-0-141-32352-7

www.greenpenguin.co.uk

Prologue

The young silver-grey wolf whined with fear as a terrifying howl rose on the icy air and echoed over the dark mountain.

'Shadow!' Storm gasped.

The fierce lone wolf, who had killed Storm's father and three litter brothers and wounded his mother, was very close.

There was a dazzling bright flash and a shower of gold sparks. Where the young wolf had been standing there now crouched a tiny Jack Russell puppy with soft brown-and-white fur, a white tail and midnight-blue eyes.

Storm hoped this disguise would protect him. He leapt towards a clump of snow-covered rocks, his tiny puppy heart beating fast. He must find somewhere to hide – and quickly.

'In here, my son,' growled a soft velvety voice.

Storm plunged deeper into the shadows and ran towards the she-wolf who was slumped beneath a rocky shelf. Yelping a greeting and wriggling his little body, he licked his mother's muzzle.

Canista reached out a large silver paw

and drew the small puppy against her thick warm fur. 'I am glad to see that you are safe and well. But you have returned at a dangerous time. Shadow wants to lead the Moon-claw pack, but the others will not follow him while you live.'

Storm's midnight-blue eyes flashed with anger. 'Then perhaps it is time for me to face him!'

'Bravely said,' Canista growled softly. 'But you are not yet strong enough to overcome him and I am still too weak from Shadow's poisoned bite to help you. Use this disguise. Go to the other world and hide. Return when your magic is stronger.' As Canista finished speaking, she gasped with pain.

'Let me help you,' Storm woofed,

blowing out a cloud of golden sparkles. They swirled around Canista's paw for a moment before sinking into her fur and disappearing.

Canista gave a sigh of relief as a tiny bit of her strength returned.

Suddenly, another fierce howl rang out, sounding much closer. Heavy paws scraped at the rocks and Storm could hear harsh breathing.

'Shadow has found your scent! Go now, Storm. Save yourself!' Canista urged.

Storm whimpered as dazzling gold sparks ignited in his short brown-and-white puppy fur and he felt the power surging through him. The gold glow around him grew brighter. And brighter . . .

Chapter
ONE

Jessica Tennant stood on the doorstep, clutching a bag of her favourite DVDs as she listened to her best friend's mum in dismay.

'I'm afraid Sheena's in bed with a nasty cold and a sore throat. I was about to call just as you arrived. It's a shame that your weekend's spoiled. You'll have to come and stay another time.'

'Oh well, she can't help being poorly,' Jessica said, trying hard to hide her disappointment. 'I'd better go then.' She had a sudden thought and held out the bag of DVDs. 'She can borrow these. Maybe they'll cheer her up. Will you tell Sheena that I hope she feels better soon?'

Sheena's mum smiled. 'That's really nice of you, Jessica. Sheena will probably ring you in a couple of days. Bye now.'

As the front door closed, Jessica's shoulders slumped. She traipsed slowly back towards her parents who were waiting, parked outside in their camper van.

Mrs Tennant looked at her daughter in surprise. 'What's happened? Why aren't you staying?' she asked.

Jessica shook her head. 'Sheena's sick, so I can't stay. We were going to have a film night and a midnight feast and everything. Now I don't know what to do,' she said miserably.

'You'll just have to come with us to the Balloon Festival,' her mum said.

Jessica pulled a face. She didn't want to go to the mega-boring old Balloon Festival with her parents. That was why she had been going to stay with Sheena in the first place. 'Can't I stay with Gran and Gramps?'

'They're on holiday, remember?' Mrs Tennant said.

'Well, what about Anjum?' Jessica said. 'Oh, no . . . she's visiting her aunt. I know! I think Gemma's at home. We could ask –'

'Hang on, Jessica,' her dad interrupted. 'I'm afraid we haven't got time to trail around all your friends' houses on the off chance that you can stay with one of them. We have to get going. The rest of The High Flyers will already be on their way. Jump in, please.'

'But . . .' Jessica's face fell as she realized that she didn't have any choice. Sighing heavily, she climbed into the back and flounced down. Leaning over, she thrust her overnight bag under the seat.

'Cheer up, Jess,' her mum said, turning round to smile as Mr Tennant pulled the van away from the kerb and headed out of town. 'I don't like to see you with such a long face.'

Jessica felt so fed up, she could feel her face getting longer and longer. It would sag right on to the floor at this rate.

'You might even have a good time. You used to think that hot-air ballooning with us was pretty exciting,' her mum said.

'Yeah! That was when I was little and before I knew that I seriously hated heights *and* found out that you had to hang around for hours when the weather's not right for flying. Which is most of the time!' Jessica said bitterly.

Mrs Tennant laughed. 'You do exaggerate, Jessica Tennant! Anyway, the forecast's pretty good for this weekend.'

Jessica wasn't cheered by this news.

Mr Tennant glanced at her in the driver's mirror. 'You should be all right at Northampton. It's a really big festival. There'll be all sorts of stalls and displays and funfair rides to go on,' he said cheerily.

'All by myself? Great,' Jessica

murmured through gritted teeth. She wished her mum and dad would stop trying to cheer her up. Nothing was going to make her feel better.

Crossing her arms, she slid down in her seat as they reached the motorway and joined the endless stream of cars and trucks. Time seemed to crawl and the next two hours felt more like two weeks.

When they eventually reached the festival, Jessica saw people everywhere, putting up stalls, erecting tents and roping off display areas. Mr Tennant parked next to a gleaming motorhome that was the size of a single-decker bus. It made their camper van look small and shabby.

'Look at that! It's even got its own satellite dish!' Jessica said, impressed despite herself.

'That's an American model. They call those RVs. I reckon you could live in that in the middle of a desert,' her dad said.

'What's an RV?' Jessica asked.

'A Recreational Vehicle. I'd love one of those!' her dad said.

'We'd have to sell the house first,' Mrs

Tennant commented drily. She got into the back of their van and began getting things out of cupboards for lunch. 'Could you go and get some water, please, Jessica?'

Jessica picked up the container and went trudging off across the car park. She really wished Sheena was here. She was missing her loads.

As she walked past an empty marquee, at the side of the car park, Jessica spotted a girl coming towards her. The girl looked about twelve, two years older than Jessica, and she was wearing a designer T-shirt and jeans.

Jessica brightened. This looked like someone she might be able to make friends with. 'Hi!' she said, as she and the girl drew level. 'Do you know where there's a water tap?'

'Do I look like I'd know?' the girl snapped.

'I suppose not,' Jessica said, thinking that she seemed very grumpy. Maybe her parents had forced her to come with them too. 'Are you here with a balloon club? I'm Jessica Tennant, by the way,' she said, introducing herself.

'I'm Gayle Young. I'm with The Cloud Racers. It's the best club ever,' the girl said, tossing her long brown hair over one shoulder.

'Dad says that about The High Flyers too,' Jessica joked. 'That's the club we belong to.'

'Huh! And I'm supposed to care?'

Gayle murmured, poking at the grass with the toe of one expensive-looking trainer.

Jessica's smile wavered, but she wasn't easily put off. 'I saw some fair rides and stuff on the way in. Maybe we could have a look around together?' she suggested.

Gayle shrugged and wrinkled her nose. 'No thanks. I'm not that keen on hanging out with younger kids. I'm already stuck with looking after Mikey – he's my little brother. I've got to go now.'

Jessica flushed as Gayle sauntered past her, disappointed that she was so unfriendly. 'Well . . . er . . . good luck in the balloon races tomorrow, anyway,' she called.

Gayle didn't bother to look round. 'We don't need luck. The Cloud Racers always win,' she drawled.

Jessica watched the older girl trudge over to the huge RV and disappear inside it. 'Oh gr-eat! Some weekend this is going to be!' she said to herself.

Jessica sighed and set off again to look for water. Suddenly, there was a flash of bright golden light and a crackle of sparks from the marquee beside her.

She frowned. Jessica had briefly glanced inside as she passed and was sure she hadn't seen anything in there. She went to check. As she had thought, there was only an upturned cardboard box and some folded chairs lying on the grass.

Then Jessica noticed the tiny brown-and-white Jack Russell puppy sitting on the box. Its fur seemed to be gleaming as if it had been sprinkled with gold dust.

'Hello. What are you doing in there all by yourself?' she crooned, walking slowly towards the puppy so as not to scare it.

'I come from far away. Can you help me, please?' the puppy woofed.

Chapter
TWO

Jessica gaped at the puppy in utter
amazement. She must be more upset by
Gayle's unfriendliness than she thought.
She'd just imagined that the tiny puppy
had spoken to her!

'I am Storm of the Moon-claw pack.
What is your name?' the puppy yapped,
looking up at her with an intelligent
expression.

'Whoa! You *can* talk!' Jessica gasped,
dropping the plastic water carrier and
taking a step backwards. 'Are you part
of an act or something?'

She quickly poked her head outside
the tent's entrance to see if one of the
festival entertainers was outside and
playing a trick on her, but there was
no one there. Jessica turned back to
Storm. He was really cute with his soft

brown-and-white fur, tiny pointed face and the brightest midnight-blue eyes she had ever seen.

Storm sat there with his ears pricked, looking at her quizzically as if expecting an answer.

'I'm J-Jessica Tennant,' Jessica found herself spluttering. 'I'm . . . here with my mum and dad for . . . for the Balloon Festival.' She bent down and tried to make herself seem smaller so as not to alarm this amazing puppy. She still couldn't quite believe this was happening to her and she didn't want Storm to run away.

Storm dipped his head. 'I am pleased to meet you, Jessica.'

'Um . . . me too.' Jessica blinked as she remembered something that Storm had just said. 'What's the Moon-claw pack?'

'It is the wolf pack once led by my father and my mother,' Storm told her proudly in a gruff little bark. 'Shadow, the evil lone wolf, killed my father and three litter brothers and left my mother injured. He wants to lead the pack, but the others will not follow him while I am alive.'

'Hang on! Did you say *wolf*? But you're a pu–'

'Please, stand back,' Storm ordered, springing down from the box.

There was another blinding flash and the air fizzed with gold sparks that rained harmlessly around Jessica and sizzled on the grass.

'Oh!' Jessica rubbed her eyes and

when she could see again she noticed
that the tiny brown-and-white puppy
had gone. In its place there stood a
magnificent young silver-grey wolf
with thick fur and huge velvety paws
that seemed far too big for his body.
Despite being young, the wolf had
large sharp teeth and a thick neck-ruff
that glittered with big golden sparkles.

Jessica looked at it warily. 'Storm?'

'Yes, it is me, Jessica. Do not be afraid,' Storm growled softly.

But before Jessica had time to get used to the majestic young wolf, there was a final gold flash and Storm reappeared as a tiny helpless brown-and-white puppy.

'Wow! You really are a wolf. That's an amazing disguise!' Jessica said.

Storm began to tremble all over and his slender white tail drooped. 'It will not save me if Shadow uses his magic to find me. I need to hide now. Can you help?' he whined.

Jessica's heart went out to him. She picked up the terrified puppy and stroked his soft little head. 'Of course I'll help you. You can live with m—'

She stopped as she remembered her
parents' strict rules about pets. 'Oh, I'm
not going to be allowed to keep you.
Back home, everyone's out all day and
most weekends too. Mum and Dad
don't think it's fair to leave a pet by
itself.'

'I understand. Thank you for your
kindness, Jessica. I will find someone
else who can help me,' Storm woofed
politely, beginning to pad away towards
the tent opening.

'Wait!' Jessica called out urgently. She wasn't ready to lose her new friend so easily. Before he'd arrived she'd been miserable. 'There must be something I can do. Maybe I could hide you in our van. Except that it's really small and Mum and Dad are bound to find you.' She had a sudden brainwave. 'Could you pretend to be a toy dog? No, that wouldn't work either, it would be too hard to stay really still and not even blink.'

Storm looked up at her with bright midnight-blue eyes. 'I can use my magic so that only you will be able to see and hear me.'

'You can make yourself invisible? Cool! Then I don't have to worry about hiding you. You can sleep with me on the sofa bed at the end of the van.'

'I would like that very much. Thank you, Jessica,' Storm woofed. He leaned up and she felt his wet nose brush her chin as he began licking her face.

Jessica smiled down at the little puppy. She felt her heart lighten as she cuddled

Storm's warm furry body. Her lonely boring weekend had just taken a most unexpected turn!

Chapter
THREE

Jessica and Storm sat at the table under the awning, which her dad had put up outside the camper van. The other members of The High Flyers had arrived now and they were all having lunch together.

At first Jessica couldn't help worrying that someone else was going to be able to see Storm sitting on her lap, but

when no one took any notice of him,
she began to relax. After checking that
she wasn't being watched, Jessica broke
off bits of her cheese roll and slipped
them secretly to Storm.

The tiny puppy chomped them up
eagerly and then jumped down on to
the grass. His tail wagged as he nosed
about, licking up every last delicious
crumb and Jessica had to try her hardest
not to giggle.

As soon as lunch was cleared away, Jessica's mum and dad and the other High Flyers began unpacking the balloon and equipment from a trailer.

Jessica had seen them do this hundreds of times. She was about to suggest to Storm that they go and have a look around, but he seemed fascinated by what was happening.

'What is that big flat coloured object lying on the grass?' Storm woofed curiously as he gambolled around with his tongue hanging out. 'Is it something to play with?'

'No! That's the club's balloon. It's made of a special light material but it's collapsed right now so you can't see the shape properly. Hey! Don't go running

about on it or you'll get a big surprise!'
she called to him in a whisper as
Storm looked like he was about to
bound on to the balloon. 'Once they've
got the burner ready, they'll light the
jets and start filling the balloon with
hot air.'

Storm's tiny forehead wrinkled in a
furry frown. 'What happens then?'

'The balloon inflates and gets really
big. It's tied down now, but if it wasn't
it would float right up in the air. As
high as the clouds.'

Storm glanced upwards, his big bright
eyes sparkling in amazement. 'Up there?'
he woofed.

Jessica nodded. She pointed to the
basket that was lying next to the
balloon. 'See that? That's where Dad

and the passengers stand when they go up in the balloon. You have to be a qualified pilot to be in charge. Dad's taken exams on flying and navigation and stuff. He's very experienced – he's won lots of races!'

'But why do humans do this?' Storm wanted to know.

'It's a hobby. That's something you do for fun,' Jessica explained.

Storm's midnight-blue eyes were as round as saucers as if he couldn't believe that anyone would want to do such a strange thing. 'Do *you* go up into the sky, Jessica?' he barked, looking very nervous.

'I used to, but I'm not very good with heights. My head goes all weird and I feel sick and wobbly,' Jessica said.

'I usually just watch from the ground or go with mum or one of the others in the support car to where the balloon lands. Sometimes I stay in the camper. But now that you're here we can have lots of fun together.'

Storm nodded, looking relieved, and seemed to lose interest in the balloons. 'Does that mean lots of walks?' he yapped, with a cheeky doggy grin.

'Definitely!' Jessica said, laughing. 'We can go for one now if you –'

There was a sudden loud hissing roar, as the burner ignited. A huge spurt of bright-yellow flame shot out and heated air began flowing into the collapsed balloon.

'Yipe!' Storm yelped, almost jumping out of his fur. He skittered sideways and his hackles rose in a ridge along his little back. 'Fire!'

Jessica felt a strange warm tingling feeling flowing down her spine as big gold sparks ignited in the tiny puppy's brown-and-white fur and his ears and tail crackled with electricity. Storm raised a front paw and a fountain of

gold glitter whooshed towards the
burner.

There was a soft *phut!* and the gas jets
went out.

Mr Tennant looked puzzled. 'That's
odd. Maybe the jets need cleaning,' he
said, trying to light them again but with
no success.

'It's OK, Storm!' Jessica whispered
hastily. 'That's what's supposed to
happen. Can you make the burner
work again, please?'

Looking rather shamefaced, Storm
sent more sparks shooting out of his
paw. The jets caught immediately and
a fresh burst of flame gushed out of
them.

'That's got it!' Mr Tennant said.

Every last gold spark disappeared from

Storm's fur, but Jessica could see that he was still frightened and wary and his little white tail was drooping.

Jessica quickly checked that everyone was busy before pretending to bend down and fiddle with her trainer. 'Don't worry. There's no danger. Dad's dead keen on health and safety,' she soothed, stroking Storm's soft little ears. 'I'm sorry. I should have explained that the burners make a scary loud noise when you're not used to them.'

Storm looked up at her trustingly and began wagging his tail.

Jessica felt a surge of affection for the brave little pup who had stood his ground and tried to help her, despite his natural fear of fire.

'That's a rubbish balloon! And the

basket's a bit small, isn't it?' said a familiar voice behind Jessica.

Gayle! Jessica shot quickly to her feet, her heart racing in case the older girl had seen her talking to Storm. But Gayle was watching the blue-purple-and-white balloon rippling as it swelled to its full size.

'It's big enough for us. Dad's won plenty of trophies in it anyway,' Jessica replied.

Gayle curled her lip. 'Sure he has,' she scoffed, making it obvious that she didn't believe Jessica for one moment. Unexpectedly, she smiled and her voice softened. 'Why don't you come and see our new balloon? It's *so* cool.'

Jessica thought about reminding Gayle that she'd said she didn't want to hang

out with younger kids, but her curiosity
got the better of her. 'OK then. We
might as well . . . um . . . I mean –
I might as well,' Jessica corrected quickly.
She would have to be a lot more careful
about keeping Storm a secret.

Gayle gave her an odd look, but then
she smirked and turned on her heel.

As Jessica followed Gayle, Storm
trotted beside her. They wove through

the other balloons and trailers and
emerged on to a big open space.

A vast black balloon in the shape of a
snarling wolf's head was just drifting
upright. It hung there, connected to an
enormous basket and tethered to the
ground. Jessica stared at it in
astonishment. She reckoned the basket
could hold about ten people. The noise
from the twin burners was really loud.

A gust of wind blew the huge black
balloon and it seemed to turn in
Jessica's direction and grin down at her
like a fierce monster.

Storm laid his ears back, shot behind
Jessica's legs and stood there trembling.

'What did I tell you? Isn't it amazing?'
Gayle said triumphantly.

'It's not bad,' Jessica said, determined

not to sound too impressed. The Cloud Racers seemed to be a much bigger club than The High Flyers. She could see about twenty people around the enormous balloon.

Jessica noticed a small boy standing with them. He looked about six years old and wore a bright-red Spider-man T-shirt.

Gayle saw where she was looking. 'That's my brother, Mikey. He's not allowed to go up in the balloon because the rules say he's too short. That's why he trails around after me when Mum and Dad are flying. He's a real pain,' Gayle grumbled.

Mikey looked over at Jessica and gave a sunny smile. He seemed really sweet. *I don't suppose it's much fun for him either,*

having to put up with a sister like Gayle,
Jessica thought.

A blonde woman stood next to
Mikey. She looked over and waved at
Gayle and Jessica. She was wearing lots
of bright make-up, a floaty pink top
and high-heeled sandals.

Gayle waved back. 'That's my mum.
Isn't she mega-gorgeous? Just like a
Hollywood film star.'

'She's very pretty,' Jessica commented, although she thought Mrs Young looked a bit too dressed up for ballooning. The other mums were wearing shorts and T-shirts and trainers.

'If you've seen enough, you can go back to your pathetic old balloon,' Gayle said cheerfully. She strolled across the grass towards her mum and little brother without a backward glance.

Jessica's jaw dropped. She'd just given Gayle another chance to be friends and had ended up being snubbed – again!

'Is there anybody as annoying as Gayle Young?' she fumed to Storm. 'Come on. I'll just go and tell my parents that I'm going for a wander around.'

'I would like that,' Storm woofed. He threw a final wary glance at the monstrous black wolf balloon before scampering after Jessica.

Chapter
FOUR

'It's a no-fly evening,' Mr Tennant said
with a sigh a couple of hours later as
he came into the camper.

Jessica was sitting reading a magazine
on the sofa bed with Storm curled up
beside her. They'd been to watch a
monster trucks' display and then a
circus workshop. Now the tiny puppy's
ears were twitching as he dozed and his

tiny paws jerked as if he was running in his dreams.

As her dad came towards her, Jessica quickly shielded Storm with her magazine and scooped him into her lap.

'Wroof!' the tiny puppy yapped in shock, instantly awake and alert.

'Sorry to disturb you, but Dad's about to squash you,' Jessica whispered as her dad sat down heavily next to her, exactly where Storm had just been lying.

'Look at this sunny weather. You'd never think the wind conditions were all wrong for flying, would you?' Mr Tennant complained.

Jessica hadn't got the heart to remind him that this often happened on ballooning weekends, which was another reason why she was sometimes so bored. But things were different for her now that she had such a special friend. Storm!

She smiled to herself as she imagined the look on her dad's face if he knew that there was an invisible magic puppy a few centimetres away from him.

'Never mind, Dad. There's still the nightglow,' she said to him, patting his arm. 'People always love seeing the balloons lit up by the burners in the dark while they're still roped to the ground.'

He smiled. 'Well, you've cheered up, I must say. I thought at one point that you were going to be Miss Glum all weekend!'

'Da-ad! I wasn't that bad!' Jessica said indignantly. She gave him a friendly shove.

He grinned. 'Says who? If your face had got any longer, you would have tripped right over it and trodden your nose into a button!'

Jessica couldn't help laughing. Her dad joined in.

After a few seconds, he wiped his eyes. 'Well, since there's not going to be a race this evening, I'm going to get the barbecue going. But first I'm going to have a cold drink and relax.' He took a copy of *Aerostat* magazine out of a nearby cupboard.

With her dad nearby, Jessica couldn't talk to Storm. She decided to take him for a short walk. 'I think I might have another look around,' she said to her dad.

Storm's ears pricked up immediately at the prospect of a walk. He jumped

down with a soft *thud* and stood bright-eyed, wagging his tail hopefully.

Jessica smiled at him, feeling all light and happy. With a twinge of guilt she realized that she wasn't missing Sheena half as much any more. She hoped her best friend wasn't feeling too poorly.

Jessica and Storm set off in a roundabout way to avoid the tethered balloons and the noise of the gas burners, which Jessica knew still upset the little puppy.

They came to the biggest bouncy castle she had ever seen. It had dozens of towers and archways and things to climb on. There was even a giant slide. Kids were laughing and screaming as they bounced around having fun.

'Go on, you wimp. Just jump straight

on to it. It's not going to bite you!'
cried an impatient voice.

It was Gayle and she was with
her little brother, still wearing his
Spider-man T-shirt.

'Gayle's with Mikey. Let's go and see
what's going on,' Jessica said to Storm.

Storm woofed softly in agreement.

'I don't want to get on it. There're
too many big kids!' Gayle's little brother
wailed, backing away.

Jessica could see that Mikey was close
to tears but trying to hide it.

'You should have thought of that
before I paid for a ticket!' Gayle
complained. 'It was out of my pocket
money too and I bet I won't get that
back. You're such a pest! Go on, Mikey.
Get up there!'

'No-oooo! Leave me alone,' Mikey
sniffled.

Jessica felt her temper rising. 'Don't
be mean, Gayle. He doesn't have to go
on if he doesn't want to!' she said.

Gayle rounded on her furiously. 'Who
asked you to stick your nose in?
Mikey's just chicken. *Cluck! Cluck!*' she
mocked, flapping her arms.

'I'm not chicken! I'm not!' Mikey
burst into tears.

Jessica's temper snapped. She glared at

Gayle. 'You're just a rotten bully!' she burst out.

Gayle narrowed her eyes. 'Who are you calling names?'

Jessica gulped as the older girl took a step towards her. Gayle suddenly seemed very tall and tough.

Storm softly growled a warning and showed his sharp little teeth. Jessica felt another warm tingling sensation flowing down her spine.

Something very strange was about to happen.

Chapter
FIVE

As Jessica watched, big gold sparks
bloomed in Storm's brown-and-white
fur, and his ears and tail fizzed with
tiny lightning flashes of power. He
raised a tiny front paw and a spray
of shimmering glitter shot out and
whizzed round Gayle like a mini-
tornado.

Gayle stopped dead as the magical

sparkles whirled faster and faster. A strange blank expression came over her face. Suddenly, she whipped round, ran forward and jumped straight up on to the bouncy castle.

Gayle did two small bounces and then on the third one she was launched high into the air before turning a triple somersault. As soon as she landed she went straight up again, somersaulted and twisted into two backflips.

The other kids stopped and watched her. They started clapping and cheering.

Mikey was no longer crying. His jaw dropped as he watched Gayle bouncing higher and higher, doing even more complicated jumps and twists.

'Aargh! What's happening?' Gayle

cried, turning over and over, her arms
windmilling madly and her legs
working as if she was riding a bike.

'Hey! You! That's not allowed! Stop
that at once!' the man in charge
ordered, storming over.

'I can't! Help!' Gayle burbled, doing a
handstand and another backflip.
Suddenly, she did an extra-big bounce.
She shot off the bouncy castle like a

cork out of a bottle and landed on her feet a few metres away from Jessica. She stood there swaying.

'I think I'm going to be sick,' she groaned, her face greenish.

'Wow! That was ace!' Mikey cried. 'Watch me, Gayle!' He seemed to have lost all his nervousness as he jumped straight on to the castle.

Gayle ignored him as she sank to the grass and sat there in a daze.

Jessica was trying hard not to laugh. 'Storm!' she scolded gently.

Storm tucked his tail between his legs. 'I am sorry. I think I used too much magic.'

Jessica smiled at him. 'Never mind. Maybe it'll teach old bossyboots Gayle a lesson. And look at Mikey.

He's really enjoying himself on the castle now! Come on, let's go for a walk.'

Storm's midnight-blue eyes widened. 'My favourite thing!'

The delicious smell of barbecued sausages wafted towards Jessica as she and Storm walked back to the camper about an hour later.

Her dad waved hello to her with a pair of tongs. He was wearing a new apron with a bright-green frog with big googly eyes on the front.

The other High Flyers were relaxing nearby in camping chairs and talking about hot-air ballooning as usual. They greeted Jessica and smiled at her as she and Storm went across to her mum,

who was sitting at the table making a
salad.

'Hello, love. Did you have a good
time?' Mrs Tennant asked.

'Yeah, we saw some people dressed
as moving statues and there was a
magician, but it's starting to get really
busy now and Storm was almost getting
trodden on –' Jessica broke off. She
couldn't believe that she'd been so
careless! But luckily her mum was busy
cutting up tomatoes and didn't seem to
have heard. 'I . . . um . . . got a bit fed
up with pushing through the crowds,'
she finished hastily.

Her mum nodded. 'I suppose people
are here for the nightglows and the
fireworks. Do you want one hot dog or
two?'

'Two please,' Jessica said at once. *One for me and one for Storm*, she thought, hoping her mum wouldn't think her greedy!

She took her plate and went to sit on the grass while she ate. 'Phew! That was close. I'm rubbish at keeping secrets. I promise I'll get better!' she said to Storm.

Storm nodded, his head on one side as he chewed up his hot dog.

After they all finished eating, Jessica helped her mum clear up. The sky turned to violet with pink streaks as the sun set and lights began coming on in the other campers and motorhomes. Her dad and the other High Flyers went to get the balloon ready for the nightglow. 'Shall we go and watch?' Jessica's mum said, drying her hands.

'OK. I'll follow you in a minute. I just want to get my shoulder bag. I think you'll be safer if you get inside it,' she whispered to Storm.

Storm jumped straight in with an eager little woof. As Jessica wandered across to the balloon display area, he settled down and poked out his head to look around.

The tethered balloons seemed a bit dull and unimpressive against the evening sky, but at a given signal all the burners were turned on. The balloons lit up, their brilliant colours shining green, gold, red and blue, like glowing Chinese lanterns.

Storm yapped excitedly, forgetting to

be nervous for a minute. 'They are brighter than the Northern Lights that ripple across the sky in the long dark winter.'

Jessica smiled wistfully, trying to imagine this wonderful sight. The other world where Storm lived as a young wolf must be very strange and wonderful.

Jessica caught sight of Gayle walking towards them. 'Uh-oh, here comes trouble,' she whispered.

As Gayle reached Jessica's mum and dad, she gave them a brilliant smile. 'Hi. Isn't it a lovely evening,' she called sweetly.

Jessica frowned. 'Gayle seems in a good mood. I wonder why.'

'Hi! I came to find you. I thought you'd be watching the nightglow,' Gayle said, smiling. She was twirling a necklace with a heart-shaped blue stone between her fingers. 'Look what my dad just bought me. Do you like it?'

'It's really pretty,' Jessica said.

Gayle smirked. 'I know. Mum and Dad are really cool. They're always buying me presents. I bet you'd love a necklace like this.'

Jessica shrugged. 'Yeah, I suppose. But I'm not that bothered. I usually only get presents on my birthday or for special occasions.'

'Poor you. What a shame that your mum and dad don't have pots of money. Anyone can tell that by looking at your scruffy old camper,' Gayle commented.

'I like our camper and it's not scruffy! It's only got a few scratches,' Jessica exclaimed, starting to get annoyed again. She made a huge effort to calm down. It just wasn't worth getting all steamed up over Gayle's pathetic comments.

'That was really weird on the bouncy

castle earlier, wasn't it?' Gayle said.

Jessica shrugged. 'I guess so,' she said.

Gayle was watching her closely. 'I
don't know what happened, but I bet
you had something to do with it. I
didn't think you had it in you,' she said
with a grudging respect.

Jessica looked at Gayle in surprise and
wondered whether she could actually
be quite good fun underneath it all.

'You just loved seeing me making a fool of myself, didn't you?' Gayle commented.

'Well, it was quite funny,' Jessica said and then wished she hadn't. Gayle scowled and the familiar mean look came over her face. She wasn't being friendly at all now – perhaps she had just been pretending.

'You think you're so cool, don't you?' Gayle spat. 'Well, no one makes fun of me and gets away with it! Just remember that!'

As Gayle stomped off, Jessica looked down at Storm in dismay. 'What do you think she means?'

Storm frowned up at her from the bag. 'It sounded as if she is going to try and get her own back.'

'Well, let her just try!' Jessica said. 'We'll be ready, won't we?'

She reached into her bag to stroke Storm's smooth warm fur and didn't notice the concerned look on his tiny face.

Chapter
SIX

'There it is! That's our balloon!' Jessica
cried early the following morning,
pointing to a bead-sized blue dot high
in the sky.

Storm sat on Jessica's lap in the back
of the The High Flyers' support car.
Kim, who owned the car, was driving.
Jessica's mum was in the passenger seat
with a map and instruments on her lap.

They were carefully tracking the
balloon, so that they would be in
exactly the right spot to help with
the landing.

'Grr-uff! Grr-uff!' Storm barked a
challenge, as he jumped up on to his
hind legs and poked his nose out of the
open window.

'Careful, Storm. Watch you don't fall out,' Jessica cautioned in a whisper.

It was 6.30 a.m. and conditions were perfect for ballooning. The clear blue sky overhead seemed filled with layers of balloons of all shapes and sizes.

'Just look at that one!' Jessica said, pointing to a giant rabbit that seemed to be waving its paw. She could see a can of soup and a big smiling head wearing earphones, but her favourite was a crocodile eating a packet of crackers.

'They are like giant creatures that roar and spit flame and chase each other!' Storm yapped. He still hadn't got used to the burners. A tiny growl rumbled in his throat whenever the hissing roar of one of them echoed on the still air.

'They're just dumb old sacks of hot air. They won't hurt you,' Jessica soothed, stroking his tense little body.

Storm gradually started to relax as Kim headed out into the countryside and drove through villages and hamlets. By the time they were nearing a patchwork of open fields, Jessica could see that The High Flyers' balloon was beginning to drift downwards.

'They'll be coming down in the fields somewhere over here,' Mrs Tennant judged, pointing at a map with her pencil. 'We should go right at the next crossroads.'

'Will do,' Kim said, concentrating hard.

'This is the tricky bit,' Jessica whispered to Storm. 'Landing can be dangerous because of power lines and stuff. Sometimes the ground wind's too strong and the basket tips over and the balloon drags it along.'

'That is not good. Someone could get hurt,' Storm woofed worriedly.

'Yes, but Dad's a brilliant pilot. You'll see. Here they come! Look!' Jessica waved to her dad, who was just a tiny figure in the basket at that moment.

Minutes later, Kim stopped the car and everyone got out. Jessica and Storm followed her mum and Kim across an unploughed field.

Suddenly, a huge black wolf balloon rose up from behind some tall trees and began descending rapidly.

Jessica ducked instinctively. 'It's The Cloud Racers! They're going to land too, but they're a bit close to our balloon!'

Storm gave a piercing whine of terror. He streaked forward and hurtled across the field in a blind panic.

'Storm!' Jessica gasped. He must have thought that the monster balloon was about to attack him.

'Where did that puppy come from?' her mum cried.

Jessica realized that Storm was so scared that he must have forgotten to stay invisible. He wouldn't be able to

use his magic to save himself without
giving himself away!

Without a second thought, Jessica
shot across the field after him.
Her heart pounded as she ran and
her trainers ate up the muddy soil.
The Cloud Racers' enormous black
balloon seemed to blot out the
entire sky and the huge basket was
barely five metres above her head.

Glancing upwards, Jessica caught a glimpse of horrified faces looking down at her.

Storm froze. He didn't seem to realize that he was right in the balloon's path. His midnight-blue eyes were like saucers and his hackles stood up along his back.

In desperation, Jessica threw herself forward. Her fingers brushed Storm's brown-and-white fur. Yes! She grabbed the tiny puppy and held him to her chest and then rolled over and over with him, as she'd been taught to do in gym lessons at school.

Just as she came to a halt beside the hedgerow at the side of the field, she bashed her knee on a large half-buried stone. 'Oh!' she gasped as a sharp pain took her breath away.

'Look out!' Jessica's mum and Kim were running across the field frantically waving their arms at the huge black balloon.

Jessica heard a shout from overhead. The powerful burners roared out and the monster wolf balloon slowed. For an agonizingly long moment, it seemed to hang in the air and then it rose just high enough to sweep over her and Storm and skim the hedge into the next field.

Jessica lay there, holding the shocked puppy. Her entire leg seemed to be aching and she couldn't move.

She saw her dad steering their

balloon to a safe landing, thirty metres away across the field. Kim ran to catch the anchor rope, while Jessica's mum ran to where Jessica lay.

'Jessica! Are you all right?' Mrs Tennant shouted anxiously.

'I'm OK, Mum. Just a bit shaken up,' Jessica cried.

Storm whined and reached up to lick Jessica's face. 'Thank you for saving me. You were very brave.'

'I wasn't really. I didn't think about it, but I just knew that I couldn't bear anything to happen to you. Quick, you'd better become invisible again. Mum's almost here!' Jessica said, wincing.

'You have hurt yourself! I will make you better,' Storm woofed.

Jessica felt the familiar tingling
down her spine as Storm opened his
mouth and huffed out a cloud of
tiny gold sparks as fine as gold dust.
The glittering mist swirled around
Jessica's leg. The pain in her knee
felt very hot for a second and then
it turned ice cold and completely
drained away like water gurgling down
a drain.

'Thanks, Storm. I'm fine now,' she said, quickly putting him on the ground and getting to her feet just as her mum reached her.

'You silly girl! Whatever made you run after that puppy? You could have been badly injured!' Mrs Tennant scolded, looking all red-faced and shaky. 'Where is the little mite, anyway?'

'It . . . er . . . ran away through the h-hedge,' Jessica gabbled hurriedly. 'It must have been a stray. Anyway, I'm all right, Mum. Don't fuss!'

'Jessica Tennant . . .' her mum said darkly, looking as if she was about to make a very big fuss indeed.

Jessica swallowed and decided that it might be sensible to change the subject.

'Hadn't we better go and help Dad and the others?' she said hastily.

With Storm haring after her, she marched across the field to where Kim, her dad and the others were dealing with the balloon.

Chapter
SEVEN

That evening, the weather was perfect
and the balloons were flying. Jessica
decided to stay behind with Storm this
time. She found a stall selling candyfloss
and then one selling pet food and
bought him a dog treat.

They went over towards the old
pavilion, where it wasn't so crowded, to
sit on the grass and eat.

'When do we go back to your home place, Jessica?' Storm woofed around a crunchy mouthful.

'Tomorrow. There's another race at 6 a.m. and then the prize-giving. After that we'll set off home,' she replied. 'I can't wait for you to meet Sheena. She's going to love you!'

'I am sorry, Jessica, but you cannot tell anyone about me. Not even your

friend.' Storm's big dewy blue eyes were serious.

'Oh.' Jessica felt disappointed that she couldn't even tell her best friend about Storm, but if that would keep him safe, she didn't mind too much.

Jessica ate the last of her candyfloss. She licked her fingers and stood up. 'Finished?' she said to Storm.

Storm nodded. He leapt to his feet and set off across the well-kept grass.

An old crisp packet blew about and Storm's bright eyes sparked with mischief as he pounced on it. Tossing his head from side to side, he tore around with the packet in his mouth.

Jessica smiled at his cute antics.

Sometimes it was hard to believe that the cheeky pup was really a majestic young silver-grey wolf who would one day lead his pack.

Suddenly, Storm stopped. He stood there quivering with concentration for a few seconds and then gave a loud yelp of terror and bolted straight into a flower bed.

Jessica stiffened. But she couldn't see what had frightened Storm. Whatever could be wrong? She raced over to the flower bed and began peering beneath a flowering bush.

'Storm? Where are you?' she called anxiously.

At first she couldn't see any sign of the little puppy, but then she spotted him. He was tucked into a tight ball in a space between two drooping branches.

'Is this a game or something? Oh, I get it. You're playing a trick on me!' she said, smiling, but then her face straightened as she saw that he was trembling all over.

'I saw a huge dog over by that tree. I think Shadow has used his magic to turn it into a wolf and send it after me!' Storm whined.

Jessica felt a clutch of fear. If Storm's enemy had found him, the tiny puppy was in terrible danger.

She glanced anxiously towards the tree and saw a woman with a big German shepherd dog on a lead. The dog saw her looking and its tongue lolled in a friendly doggy grin.

'Those dogs look a bit like wolves, but that one seems gentle,' Jessica whispered uncertainly as the woman and her dog came closer. 'How will I know if it's under a magic spell?'

'It will have fierce pale eyes and extra-long sharp teeth,' Storm whined nervously.

Jessica looked at the German shepherd again. 'It doesn't look like that. I think it's OK.'

Storm crawled forward with his belly close to the ground and his tail between his legs. He peered through the drooping branches at the big dog and Jessica saw him gradually relax.

'You are right. I am mistaken this time. But if Shadow finds me, he *will* use his magic to hunt me down.'

Jessica felt a surge of protectiveness. She bent down and picked Storm up as he crept out from under the bush. She could feel his little heart beating fast against her fingers. 'I hope that horrible Shadow never finds you and then you can come home with me and stay forever!'

Storm looked up at her. 'One day, I must return to my own world to help

my mother and become leader of the Moon-claw pack. Do you understand that, Jessica?' he yapped gently.

Jessica nodded, but she didn't want to think about that right now. 'You've had a nasty scare. Let's go back to the camper and spend some quiet time together,' she said, changing the subject.

Storm reached up to lick her chin. 'I would like that,' he barked.

Jessica carried Storm to the car park. As they came in sight of their camper, the door opened and a girl peered out. After a quick look around, she climbed down and hurried away.

'That was Gayle. What's she doing in our camper?' Jessica wondered.

Storm frowned. 'I do not know.'

'Maybe Mum came back to fetch

something and Gayle was chatting to her,' Jessica said, knowing how Gayle was always careful to be on her best behaviour around adults.

But when she went inside, she saw that the camper was empty.

Storm stood with his head on one side.

'What is it?' Jessica asked him.

'Something is different . . .' Tiny gold sparks began twinkling in Storm's fur and his wet brown nose began to glow like a gold nugget. With a triumphant woof he jumped up on to the back seat and began rooting about behind a cushion. A moment later, he emerged holding something in his mouth.

It was a gold necklace with a blue, heart-shaped stone.

Jessica recognized it. 'That's Gayle's new necklace. She must have put it there. But why?'

'I think I know why!' Storm barked and then he pricked up his ears. 'Someone is coming!' He picked up the necklace and dashed out of the open door with it in his mouth.

Puzzled, Jessica followed hard on his heels. 'Storm? What's going on? Where are you go—' she started to ask and then stopped herself quickly as she saw Gayle and her mum standing there.

Mrs Young was wearing a frilly blue dress and high heels. She had one arm round Gayle, who was dabbing at her eyes with a tissue.

'I want a word with you, young lady!' Mrs Young said at once. 'Gayle's lost her new necklace and she thinks that you might know something about it!'

'Me?' Jessica said, almost speechless.

Gayle grinned slyly. 'Don't try and look innocent,' she sniffled. 'I know you took it.'

Jessica couldn't believe her ears. 'I couldn't care less about your stupid necklace. I didn't take it!' she burst out.

'Huh! You would say that!' Gayle sneered. 'I bet you've hidden it inside the camper. Come on, Mum, let's go inside and look for it.'

'Now wait just a minute!' said a deep voice behind them.

'Dad!' Jessica gave a cry of relief as her dad stepped forward.

'I heard all that,' he said. 'And I can assure you that my daughter's no thief.

If Jessica says she didn't take the
necklace, I believe her.'

Mrs Young gave him a charming
smile. Her teeth were very white against
her bright-pink lipstick. 'In that case,
you won't mind if we come into your
camper and have a look.'

'I certainly do mind! Gayle's probably
dropped that necklace somewhere. I
suggest you go and look for it, before
you come here making wild

accusations,' Mr Tennant said calmly.

'Well! If that's your attitude,' Mrs Young said indignantly, drawing herself up. 'You haven't heard the last of this, I assure you. Come along, Gayle.'

Gayle looked as if she was about to protest, but she turned and hurried after her.

As Mrs Young stalked towards her motorhome in her high heels, she suddenly stopped. 'What's that glinting in the grass?' she said, bending down to pick something up. She turned to Gayle. 'It's your necklace! You must have dropped it, just like Mr Tennant said.'

'But I don't get it! I put it under . . . I mean . . . I . . . um . . . didn't . . .' Gayle stammered in confusion.

'You've made me look a complete

idiot!' Mrs Young fumed, marching Gayle up the steps of the RV. 'What have you been up to? And you'd better tell me the truth, or you'll be grounded!'

The door closed firmly and silence fell. Jessica guessed that Gayle was getting a really severe telling-off. She turned back to her dad. 'Thanks for sticking up for me, Dad.'

'No problem,' he said, giving her shoulder a squeeze. 'You haven't got a mean bone in your body, Jessica Tennant. But it was a good thing we got back here in time.'

Just as her dad went into the van, Storm came out from underneath the camper and lolloped up to Jessica.

'Thanks, Storm. That was a brilliant

idea to drop Gayle's necklace over by the RV. It really turned the tables on her!'

'You are welcome, Jessica. I do not think she will be making any more trouble,' he yapped happily.

Chapter
EIGHT

Jessica woke up early on Sunday morning. Pale lemon sunlight was just pushing through the crack in the camper's curtains.

Storm was lying next to her. He wagged his little tail as she stroked him, and snuggled back under a fold of the warm duvet with a contented sigh.

Jessica felt wide awake. Leaving Storm

lying there, she carefully climbed
over him and dressed in shorts and a
T-shirt. After boiling the kettle, she
took her mum and dad a cup of tea
in bed.

'Thanks, love. You're an early bird
today!' Mr Tennant sat up looking
sleepy-eyed and with his hair all tousled.
'You're not making breakfast too, are
you?' he asked hopefully.

Jessica took the hint. 'Eggs on toast?'

By the time they were clearing away the cups and plates, the other High Flyers had arrived. Kim had bad news.

'It's going to be another no-fly day,' she announced. 'So the winning times have been worked out from Friday's and Saturday's flights. We're in second place. The Cloud Racers are first.'

Mr Tennant nodded. 'Ah well, that's how it goes,' he said good-naturedly. 'It's a shame we won't get a chance for another flight. But there'll still be a balloon tether before we pack away for good.'

'That's when the balloons are roped to the ground and just hover a few centimetres in the air. No balloon monsters high in the sky to scare you today then,' Jessica explained in a whisper to Storm.

Outside in the enclosure, cars and trailers had drawn up and the grass was already covered with acres of brightly coloured nylon. Jessica could see that The Cloud Racers' basket lay on its side. The burners were going and the huge black wolf face was almost fully inflated.

She and Storm were standing with her mum and dad when Gayle's parents hurried up to them. Mrs Young was holding Mikey's hand.

'Have you seen Gayle?' Mr Young asked Jessica.

Jessica shook her head, puzzled. 'No,

I haven't seen her since yesterday.'

She noticed that Mrs Young looked different and then realized why. Gayle's mum was in jeans and a crumpled T-shirt and she wasn't wearing make-up. Her eyes looked puffy as if she'd been crying.

'Is something wrong?' Mrs Tennant asked her gently.

'It's Gayle. She's missing,' Mrs Young said in a wobbly voice. 'We had a bit of a row about this necklace business. I thought at first that she'd gone off somewhere sulking by herself – she's done it before. But it's been over an hour now and I'm starting to get really worried.'

'I'll help you look for her,' Jessica offered at once.

'That's very nice of you, especially after the way Gayle behaved,' Mr Young said.

'Anyone can make a mistake,' Jessica said generously.

'Let's all spread out and look around,' Mr Tennant suggested.

'Good idea. I'll look over here,' Jessica said, walking off with Storm. She

waited until her mum and dad
had gone in opposite directions and
then turned to Storm. 'Do you think
you can pick up Gayle's scent?' she
asked.

'I will try,' Storm woofed.

Scampering over to the Youngs'
RV, he began nosing about in the
grass.

Jessica followed him and watched as
he worked his way back and forth.
Moments later, his head came up. 'This
way,' he yapped triumphantly.

Jessica ran after him as he headed
towards the line of tethered balloons.
The Cloud Racers' huge black
balloon and basket were floating a
few centimetres above the ground.
Two of the club members were

standing with their backs to the balloon.

Jessica caught a sudden movement from the corner of her eye. A slim figure suddenly dashed out from behind a van and quick as a flash scrambled unseen into the huge basket.

'It's Gayle!' Jessica gasped, rushing forward with Storm at her heels.

As she ran up to the balloon, she saw Gayle lean over, unhook a guy rope and drop it to the ground. The basket wobbled and tipped at a crazy angle.

The two club members turned. They realized what was happening and quickly grabbed a rope each, but the balloon began to rise slowly as Gayle unhooked another rope and threw it down.

'Gayle, don't!' Jessica cried.

Gayle glared at her. 'What do you care? You don't like me. Everyone hates me!' The balloon rose up higher, straining for freedom.

'I don't hate you, and your mum and dad are really worried about you. Just stay still and let the team get you down,' Jessica pleaded.

Gayle bit her lip and looked as

if she might be starting to believe Jessica.

'Gayle! What on earth do you think you're doing? Get down from there!' Mr Young ordered, as he, his wife and Mikey ran towards the balloon.

Then everything happened at once.

The club members, already on tiptoe and trying to hold down the balloon, were lifted off their feet. They dropped to the ground as the black balloon rose into the air, trailing ropes and taking Gayle up with it.

Jessica saw the balloon ripple as if it was caught in a side wind. It lurched sideways and the wolf face seemed to leer as it started to collapse.

Gayle screamed and clung on to the basket.

Jessica gasped in horror. The whole thing was going to come crashing down!

Chapter
NINE

Time seemed to stand still.

Huge gold sparks bloomed in Storm's brown-and-white fur and his ears fizzed with power. He shot into the air, trailing a comet's tail of sparkles and landed in the basket next to Gayle.

Jessica saw a burst of flame shoot out of the gas jets. Hot air flowed into the

balloon, which swelled out and righted
itself. At the same time a gush of
gold sparkles erupted in the basket, and
ropes snaked downwards towards the
ground.

Eager hands reached for them and
they were quickly secured. People ran
to help and the balloon was drawn
downwards until the basket rested on
the grass.

Jessica saw Storm leap out and streak towards her.

Gayle's dad leapt into the basket and gave his daughter a huge hug. 'Are you all right, love? I was terrified that you were going to be hurt. Thank goodness that you had the sense to work the burner and throw down those extra ropes.'

Gayle was white-faced. She didn't seem to know whether to laugh or cry. 'Burner? But I . . .' she stammered shakily.

But her dad wasn't listening. He helped Gayle climb out of the basket and one of the club members reached forward to steady her. Everyone cheered and clapped.

Gayle hung her head and chewed at

her lip. 'Thanks, everyone. I-I didn't mean that to happen. I'm glad that no one got hurt because of me.'

Jessica could see that, for once, Gayle really meant it.

She looked down at Storm who stood beside her. Every last spark had faded from his fur. She wished she could cuddle him, but there were too many people around for her to pick him up.

'That was incredibly brave of you to light the burner, Storm. I know how fire terrifies you,' she whispered.

'I am just glad that Gayle is safe. But I do not think I will ever grow to like hot-air balloons,' he barked.

Jessica noticed Gayle looking at her in a very strange way. She realized that the older girl had heard her whispering to Storm!

Gayle smiled knowingly and then she shrugged. 'Weird things keep happening when you're around, Jessica. I'd love to know what's been going on, but I guess I never will. Keep your secrets. It's fine by me. And thanks for trying to help me. I'm sorry for being such a pain.

Can we start all over again and try to be friends?'

'I'd like that,' Jessica replied, pleased.

'Cool! Why don't you come over to our RV? You haven't seen inside, have you. It's got a huge shower room and a TV and everything.'

Jessica smiled. Gayle would never change, but at least she was trying to be a lot nicer now. 'OK, thanks. I'd love to see around it,' she said.

Gayle beamed at her. She reached for Mikey's hand before walking off with her parents. 'See you in a minute, Jessica.'

With the excitement over, people began dispersing. Suddenly, Storm whimpered and began trembling all over. He took off like a rocket and

pelted for a clump of thick bushes a few metres away.

'I'll . . . I'll be right back!' Jessica gabbled to her mum. She hurtled after the terrified puppy, a dreadful suspicion rising in her mind.

She spotted three dogs running towards the bushes from the opposite direction. They had fierce pale eyes and extra-long sharp teeth. Shadow had put

a spell on them. They were here for
Storm.

As Jessica pushed her way into the
centre of the bushes there was a
dazzling flash of bright gold light.

Storm stood there, a tiny brown-and-
white Jack Russell puppy no longer.
He was a majestic young wolf with
thick silver-grey fur. A thousand
tiny gold diamonds sparkled in his
neck-ruff. Beside him stood an older
she-wolf with a gentle expression on
her face.

At that moment, Jessica knew that
Storm must leave her. Her throat
clenched with sadness, but she forced
herself to be brave. 'Save yourself,
Storm!' she cried.

'Be of good heart, Jessica. You have

been a loyal friend,' Storm said in a deep velvety growl.

There was a final burst of intense gold light, and a silent explosion of sparks crackled down around Jessica. Storm and his mother faded and were gone.

There was a growl of rage as the fierce dogs burst through the bushes. Seeing that Storm had disappeared, their eyes and teeth instantly returned to normal and they fled.

Jessica felt stunned. It had all happened so fast. Her heart was aching, but at least she'd had a chance to say goodbye. Storm was safe and she hoped that one day he would be able to stay in his own world and lead the Moon-claw pack.

Tears pricked her eyes as she slowly began walking back towards the car park. Jessica knew she would never forget her wonderful adventure with Storm.

She thought of Sheena and hoped she was feeling better. Jessica decided to buy her a cuddly toy to cheer her up. Then she smiled as she saw Gayle waiting for

her. Perhaps she'd get Gayle one too. A cute toy puppy for them both.

After all, she thought, *everyone should have their own magic puppy*.

Win a Magic Puppy goody bag!

The evil wolf Shadow has ripped out part of Storm's
letter from his mother and hidden the words so that magic puppy
Storm can't find them.

Storm needs your help!

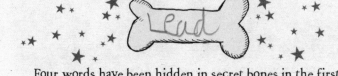

Four words have been hidden in secret bones in the first
four Magic Puppy books. Find the hidden words and put them
together to complete the message from Storm's mother.
Send it in to us and each month we will put every correct message
in a draw and pick out one lucky winner, who will receive
a Magic Puppy gift – definitely worth barking about!

Send the hidden message, your name and address on a postcard to:
Magic Puppy Competition
Puffin Books
80 Strand
London WC2R 0RL
Good luck!

puffin.co.uk

Magic Puppy

A New Beginning
9780141323503

Muddy Paws
9780141323510

Cloud Capers
9780141323527

Star of the Show
9780141323534

puffin.co.uk

Coming Soon

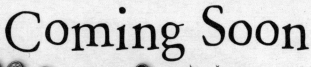

A little puppy,
a sprinkling of magic,
a forever friend.

puffin.co.uk

If you like
Magic Puppy,
you'll love

Magic
Kitten

A Summer Spell
9780141320144

Classroom Chaos
9780141320151

Star Dreams
9780141320168

Double Trouble
9780141320175

Moonlight Mischief
9780141321530

A Circus Wish
9780141321547

Sparkling Steps
9780141321554

A Glittering Gallop
9780141321561

Seaside Mystery
9780141321981

Firelight Friends
9780141321998

Sparkling Steps
9780141321554

A Puzzle of Paws
9780141322018

A Christmas Surprise
9780141323237

Picture Perfect
9780141323480

A Splash of Forever
9780141323497